ISBN 978-1-331-39194-4
PIBN 10183751

This book is a reproduction of an important historical work. Forgotten Books uses state-of-the-art technology to digitally reconstruct the work, preserving the original format whilst repairing imperfections present in the aged copy. In rare cases, an imperfection in the original, such as a blemish or missing page, may be replicated in our edition. We do, however, repair the vast majority of imperfections successfully; any imperfections that remain are intentionally left to preserve the state of such historical works.

For support please visit www.forgottenbooks.com

1 MONTH OF
FREE
READING

at

www.ForgottenBooks.com

By purchasing this book you are eligible for one month membership to ForgottenBooks.com, giving you unlimited access to our entire collection of over 1,000,000 titles via our web site and mobile apps.

To claim your free month visit:

www.forgottenbooks.com/free183751

English
Français
Deutsche
Italiano
Español
Português

www.forgottenbooks.com

Mythology Photography **Fiction**
Fishing Christianity **Art** Cooking
Essays Buddhism Freemasonry
Medicine **Biology** Music **Ancient**
Egypt Evolution Carpentry Physics
Dance Geology **Mathematics** Fitness
Shakespeare **Folklore** Yoga Marketing
Confidence Immortality Biographies
Poetry **Psychology** Witchcraft
Electronics Chemistry History **Law**
Accounting **Philosophy** Anthropology
Alchemy Drama Quantum Mechanics
Atheism Sexual Health **Ancient History**
Entrepreneurship Languages Sport
Paleontology Needlework Islam
Metaphysics Investment Archaeology
Parenting Statistics Criminology
Motivational

Young Folk's Library of Choice Literature

STORIES

OF

MINNESOTA

GEO. F. FORSTER

Superintendent of Schools, Fairfax, Minn.

"The Spartans did not inquire how many the enemy are, but where they are."

EDUCATIONAL PUBLISHING COMPANY

BOSTON

NEW YORK   CHICAGO   SAN FRANCISCO

THE INDIAN MAID'S WAR SONG.

Hark! the war song — the shouting — I hear the shrill sound;
 They raise the red tomahawk out of the ground:
 In the van of the battle my warrior must go;
Like the blood-thirsty panther he'll steal on his foe.

Yet with love his bold heart is still beating for me,
 With a feeling like mine which death only can sever;
In kindness it flows as the sweet sugar-tree,
 And akin to the aspen it trembles forever.
     — *Sioux Poem in Dublin University Magazine.*

CONTENTS.

FOREWORD.

The history of the struggle of the pioneer and yeoman of early Minnesota, though it is an inland state, carved out of the Louisiana and Northwest Territories, reads like the story of many a state won along the coast. The battles of the settlers with soil and savage, the energy and thrift later displayed by her citizens, or their patriotism when war called to action — these things are not new, nor indeed remarkable, when their frequency is counted. But a knowledge of the struggles and their incident deeds of courage, necessary to planting a new world, and especially a knowledge of what was necessary to a conquest of America, is of value to youth. And surely it is more fitting that the western boys and girls should finish their school-days with a knowledge of the historical facts in the rise of their own states to eminence, rather than that they be acquainted only with the story of the Pilgrims of Massachusetts or the Cavaliers of Virginia.

With facts that interest him, moreover, the pupil does better work in his reading classes, than with facts that do not; and, the point of view being nearer, he will be more interested, if he lives in Minnesota, in the history of Minnesota than in the history of Lapland or of the Dutch in New York.

The following pages have been written partly for my own classes, partly for publication, and all with an abundant love for our growing Commonwealth and the children of its splendid schools. Intended, primarily, for seventh grade pupils, this brief account may well serve its purpose in sixth or eighth grades.

Credit, where due, has been given in the pages that follow.

FAIRFAX.   G. F. F.

STATE FLAG OF MINNESOTA.

STORIES OF MINNESOTA.

THE INDIAN'S STORY.

Menard.

Listen to the story of the Huron youth, Owasicut:

By the falling waters of the Oswego, in the country of the Iroquois, we had dwelt in peace and plenty. Deep among the trees of the forest lay our village, and not far off the sandy shores of the big water of the Ontarios. It was there we caught our fish, and along its shores we hastened, when the war loving Iroquois dug up the buried tomahawk and forced us to flee.

We came to the protection of the peaceful Ottawas and gave our name to the Lake-of-the-Bay. But the "great want" drove us again towards the setting sun; sent us to the country of the Ojibways

by the shoies of Mitchi Sawgyegan.* Some of us
followed the sun even to the beautiful Minnesota,
"the sky-tinted watei," and met with the fieice
young waiiiois of the Dakotahs, called by the Chippewas, †Nadouessioux, which means enemies.

The waiiiois of the Dakotahs had not seen such
guns and knives and axes as those of oui biaves, and
made fiiends with oui band, and gave us land,— an
island in the middle of the gieat Fathei of Wateis,
— smoked a calumet and called oui young men
biotheis. Few the days and nights we stayed and
weie called theii biotheis, the biotheis of the
Dakotahs. They did not love us, it was oui guns
and knives they loved. In angei we jouineyed up
against the stieam of the Chippewas and built oui
tepees again by the Big Sea, and gave the place a
name, Chaguamegon.

Sullenly we dwelt, and the moons weie but few
that passed befoie theie came seeking us heie the
black-iobed chief, Menaid. In that countiy far
away towaids the day-dawn, by the lake of the

*Michigan.   † Ojibways and Chippewas are the same tiibe.

Hurons, we had known him. He had taught the boys and the squaws the goodness of his Great Spirit and given the sick men medicine; but revenge was working among the warriors of the Hurons, revenge against the Sioux. Why should not we, with our guns and sharper axes, why should not we be master and the Nadouessioux slave?

Father Menard taught us that revenge was for his Great Spirit only, but we were sullen men and would not listen, and bade him silence; but Father Menard was not a coward man and would not be still, and cried, "Are we to serve the Great Spirit only when there is nothing to suffer and no risk of life?" So one day the black-robed chief, going out in his canoe came not back again, but Eagle Feather, who was his companion, came back alone and said around that the good father had been lost in the many paths where he had landed. And the sullen warriors said, "It is well he comes no more."

And one hundred of the bravest of our young men saw the time was good, and we went again the Dakotahs and met them near the village of their chief, Crow Wing. But fearful is the twang of the bow-string of the Dakotahs. The air was filled with swift-flying arrows, and even while they ran from us they turned their faces and fired again. As many Huron braves of my companions fell whether our enemies stood or ran. So the Dakotahs drove us into the marshes, and bitten by the stinging flies, and burning under the fire of the sun, we lay in quiet until the night. But again the foe was better than were we, for they had laid thongs of beaver skins, hung with bells, in our path. We stumbled on the bells and quickly the Sioux had cut us down, all but one. Me they made captive and brought into the village.

The Sioux are like Iroquois, fierce and quarrelsome, and always at war. They live in many great villages along the Father of Waters and are leagued together in one strong nation. So do they call themselves Dakotahs. Of planting and cultivating the earth they have no knowledge like as we have,

but live on the wild oats and wild rice of the
marshes. Nor is their language like the Huron,
smooth and flowing, but rough, guttural and coarse.

I like them not at all, but I must stay here.

And often while I stay, I think of the good white
father who loved his Huron children, and first
among us tried to teach us of the Great Spirit.

TA-TANKA-NAZIN.
(A Sioux Chief.)

THE INDIAN'S STORY.

Du Lhut.

It was in the Moon of Falling Leaves a white man came to trade among the villages of the Sioux. From Quebec he journeyed in a canoe with other traders, and had the name Du Lhut. The white man brought the tribesmen of the Sioux many gifts of beads and weapons, and told of the great white chief who dwelt a long way off, across a mighty water, in a country he named France; a noble pale face, who loved the braves of the Dakotahs, the old men and the young men, and their squaws and their pappooses, and called them all his children. At Mah-to-wa, upon a tree, he cut the totem of his chief, and raised the arms of France. Many councils he held with the warriors of the village, and in one he spoke in this wise, standing tall and black against the moonlight:

"O Chief, many scalps hang at Crow Wing's belt; he is brave and noble. The white men and the Dakotahs have smoked the calumet together, and the great chief, Crow Wing, has heard it said before the council-fire of his braves, 'The pale face loves his brother.' Many presents has he given the braves and young men of the Dakotahs, and after many smokes he is allowed to push his light canoe along your waters. Yet Crow Wing can see the white man knows not the road unless he gives him guides to take him on his way. On the great Mississippi, the father of the waters, in the hunting grounds of the Dakotahs, the white man would meet his friend, the black-robed medicine man* of the pale faces. But the way is dark, he will lose himself in the forest and see his brother, Crow Wing, never again."

Then the white man, Faffart, told in Sioux the speech of Du Lhut; but I, Owasicut, already knew it; for many suns before Du Lhut had seen the country of the Sioux, Father Menard journeyed to their land and paddled on the waters of the Miss-

---

* Hennepin, it was reported, was on the Lower Mississippi.

issippi. I had seen him then and learned his speech, and he had taught us, as many winters before he had done in the country of the Ottawas, by the Great Lake of the Hurons.

Crow Wing took his long pipe from his mouth, blew the white smoke up into the heavens and answered: "The white chief speaks well, and Crow Wing will send his young men to guide his white brother to the great Father of Waters, that he may return again for beaver and otter."

But Crow Wing did not send his young men as he promised. For one of the two canoes of Du Lhut he sent a captive Chippewa, and for the other his Huron prisoner, me, Owasicut. With many skins of beaver packed upon the backs of white and red men, Owasicut led the way in silence through the forest, from the village of Mah-to-wa; guns and powder had the white man left with Crow Wing for his beaver pelts. There were as many that journeyed through the forest as the fingers of Owasicut's hands, and two of them were red men.

Soon the watei loomed befoie the white men and
theii guides, the Big Sea Water, and on the sandy
beach, beside the log tepee Du Lhut had built, the
canoes lay waiting. Du Lhut stood looking at the
place and said, "It is the far end of the lake, and so
it shall be called Fond du Lac."

Then said Du Lhut to the white man who spoke
the language of the Dakotahs, "Faffart, do you take
in youi canoe two packeis and the Chippewa, whilst
the iest go with the Sioux in the othei."

"Owasicut is not a Sioux, Monsieui, a Huion is
Owasicut. When not yet a waiiioi, I leained the
white man's language among the Ottawas when
Fathei Menaid was alive and taught us."

"Menaid? Well I knew him. He did laboi
faithfully among the ied men; and you say the good
fathei is dead? When was it? for I saw him a few
months since."

"But as many moons ago as I have eyes, O pale
face, he wandered away and came not back."

"Rest his soul in peace! And may angels

guaid those men of stiength and couiage who aie
tiying for a passage to the South Sea, by this same
Fathei of Waters, for which we aie seaiching.
Gieat hope lies in my heait that I may meet them,
theiefoie let us hasten."

Swiftly rushed the biich canoes ovei the wateis of
the Big Sea, and when the sun had slept a little,
Owasicut had led them into the Nemitsakout. On
its banks the white men stopped and iested until the
sun once moie awoke. When the white chief had
waked, Owasicut set off, and guided up against the
stieam the canoes and told the tiaveleis of theii
jouineys as he woiked.

"The sun will sleep once moie and iise again,
and in a little time the pale face can paddle no moie.
Then must he walk as far as he can see, and carry
his canoe to wheie anothei iivei iises in a lake and
by its wateis shall we come into the gieat Fathei of
Wateis."

And as Owasicut had said, so it happened.

Not many times the sun had slept and wakened,

when, from passing Chippewas, it was learned a
hunting party of the lower Sioux had passed below
in the Mississippi, and with them white men; one a
black-robed, smooth-faced man, the others bearded,
hairy trappers; and that the black-robed chief was
wakan (of a mystical, wizard-like nature). Then it
was that Owasicut left the white men and went back
among his people, but he forgets not the brave
white chief who, first among the Sioux, had made
them friendly to the white men — the white men who
first of their people were allowed on the bosom of
the great Father of Waters in the country of the
Dakotahs. I am an old man now, but I forget not
Sieur Du Lhut.

FATHER LOUIS HENNEPIN, RECOLLECT.
1680.

About the year 1650 there was born to poor people in the little town of Ath, in Holland, a boy baby. He was duly christened in the little church of the town by the good curé, when his god-mother gave him the name Louis, after Louis XIV., the Grand Monarch, who was then reigning in France.

As the lad grew up he early displayed a roving disposition and manifested an intense desire to visit some of the lands far away over the ocean to the west. At that time settlement of the French lands was being vigorously prosecuted by "le Grand Monarch," and the wonders of the new country were the all-absorbing topic of the little town of Ath. What wonder, then, that Louis felt resistlessly drawn toward Quebec and the western colonies!

But his parents consecrated him to the priesthood,
and for a time, at least, he had to stifle his longings
and patiently wait events. Every opportunity, however, that offered itself to hear stories of adventure
and hair-breadth escape was eagerly snapped up,
and we find him stealing away to sailors' taverns
and the loitering places of adventurers, and spending days, regardless of loss of time or meals, in
listening behind the doors.

At last comes his opportunity. The Superior of
the Order of St. Francis, to which he belongs,
requires him to immediately embark for Canada, and
in company with La Salle and other explorers, he is
soon afloat and bound for the New World (1676).
After sojourning for a short period at Quebec, the
adventure-loving Franciscan is permitted to go to a
mission station on or near the site of the present
town of Kingston, Ont. Here there was much to
gratify his love of novelty, and he passed considerable time in rambling among the Iroquois of New
York. Then a little later he is encamped with

La Salle's party on the Niagara River, waiting for spring to break the ice in the Great Lakes before starting West, whiling away the hours, meanwhile, in studying the manners and customs of the Seneca Indians, and in admiring the sublimest of God's handiworks, Niagara Falls.

Passing hurriedly over their stormy voyage, we lift the curtain upon the party again at Fort Crevecœur on the Illinois River, just as Father Hennepin and two others are leaving the fort in a frail Indian canoe to ascend the Mississippi. He has himself written the narrative of his voyage and despite the fact that there are those who are inclined to think he prevaricates at times and often exaggerates, we will let him tell his own tale. He writes:

"Our prayers were heard, when on the 11th of April, 1680, about two o'clock in the afternoon, we suddenly perceived thirty-three bark canoes, manned by a hundred and twenty Indians, coming down with very great speed, on a war party, against the Miamis, Illinois, and Maronas. These Indians surrounded us, and while at a distance, discharged some arrows at us, but as they approached our canoe, the old men seeing us with the Calumet of peace in our hands, prevented the young men from killing us. These savages, leaping from their canoes, some on land, others into the water, approached us with frightful cries and yells, and as we made no resistance, being only three against so great a number, one of them wrenched our Calumet from our hands, while our canoe and theirs were tied to the shore.

"As we did not understand their language, we took a little stick, and by signs which we made on the sand, showed them that their enemies, the Miamis, whom they sought, had fled across the Mississippi to join the Illinois. When they saw themselves discovered and unable to surprise their enemies, three or four old men, placing their hands on my head, wept in a mournful tone.

"With a spare handkerchief I had left I wiped away their tears, but they would not smoke our

Calumet. They made us cioss the iivei while all shouted with teais in theii eyes; they made us iow befoie them, and we heaid yells capable of stiiking the most iesolute with teiioi. Aftei landing oui canoe and goods, pait of which had alieady been taken, we made a fiie to boil oui kettle, and we gave them two laige wild tuikeys which we had killed.

" Then the Indians, having called an assembly to delibeiate what they weie to do with us, the two head chiefs of the paity appioaching, showed us by signs that the waiiiois wished to tomahawk us. This compelled me to go to the wai chiefs with one young man, leaving the othei by oui piopeity, and thiow into theii midst six axes, fifteen knives and six fathom of oui black tobacco; and then biinging down my head, I showed them with an axe that they might kill me, if they thought piopei. This piesent appeased many individual membeis, who gave us some beavei to eat, putting the thiee fiist moisels into oui mouths, accoiding to the custom of the countiy; and blowing on the meat which was veiy hot, before putting the bark dish before us to let us eat what we liked. We spent the night in anxiety, because, before retiring, they had returned us our peace Calumet.

"Our two boatmen were resolved to sell their lives dearly, and to resist if attacked; their arms and swords were ready. As for my own part, I resolved to let myself be killed without any resistance, as I was going to announce to them a God who had been foully accused, unjustly condemned, and cruelly crucified, without showing the least aversion to those who put him to death. We watched in turn, in our anxiety, so as not to be surprised asleep. The next morning, a chief named Na-ra-to-ba asked for the peace Calumet, filled it with the bark of the red willow, *killiki-nnick*, and we all smoked. It was then signified that the white men were to return with them to their villages. . . .

" I found it difficult to say my office before these Indians. Many seeing me move my lips, said in a disturbed tone of voice, *wakan de* (wonderful).

Michael, all out of countenance, told me, that if I continued to say my breviary, we should all three be killed, and le Picard begged me at least to pray apart, so as not to provoke them. I followed the latter's advice, but the more I concealed myself the more I had the Indians at my heels; for when I entered the wood, they thought I was going to hide some goods underground, so that I knew not on what side to turn to pray, for they never let me get out of sight. . . . They thought the breviary was a spirit which taught me to sing for their diversion; for these people are naturally fond of singing."

Many other things connected with the good Father were *wakan*, likewise: his chalice, his compass, his writing on paper, a certain iron pot with feet like the paws of a lion, were all "magic" or "supernatural" to the untutored savages.

Hennepin was the first white man to visit the Falls of the Mississippi, where now stands the beautiful metropolis of the Northwest, Minneapolis, and he it was who named the falls, calling it after his patron saint, St. Anthony of Padua. While with a hunting party of Sioux on the Mississippi below the falls, Hennepin was met by Du Lhut and Faffart, who had come down from their trading-post at Fond du Lac on Lake Superior.

After about six months' stay among the Sioux of the Upper Mississippi, Hennepin, with his compauions, eight Frenchmen in all, returned to the fort on the Illinois, and from there to France, to publish the wonderful history of his explorations.

CARVER.

Just west of Minneapolis, you will find on your state map Carver County, named after Jonathan Carver, who came to Minnesota, or, as it was then called, Louisiana, on a tour of exploration in 1766, ten years before the signing of the Declaration of Independence. Carver came from Connecticut, and was thirty-four years old when he came West.

When, in his fifteenth year, his father died, he immediately began to think upon his future, and although his father had been a captain in the army of King William, Jonathan decided he wanted to be a doctor. In three years, however, he had changed his mind, and we find him an ensign in the English army fighting against the French in the colonies.

History says he was wounded at Lake George in 1757, and nearly lost his life.

When the French had been defeated, Jonathan came West with a number of traders, following the usual route, *via* the Great Lakes and the Straits of Mackinaw, and arrived at Green Bay, Wisconsin, the 18th of September, 1866. By canoe he journeyed up Fox River and down the Wisconsin into the Mississippi at Prairie du Chien. Near this place the traders camped for the winter, while Carver, with two companions — a Canadian voyager and a Mohawk Indian — proceeded farther up the Mississippi.

Stopping one day near the beautiful Lake Pepin, he went up the bank of the river to look around while the attendants were getting ready his dinner. Not far from the river he saw a large, level plain, and in the plain an earthwork large enough to cover five thousand men: four feet in height, nearly a mile long and circular in form, its flanks touched the river bank. It had evidently been built for centuries, for it was covered with grass and trees, and it could not have been raised by the untutored Indian; it was too regular and fashioned with too much military skill, every angle being, even then, visible. A ditch had once existed about the whole embankment, and the structure overlooked the entire country for considerable distance around. It was probably a monument of the pre-historic Mound Builders, whose works, we shall find, are to be seen in many places in Minnesota.

Lake Pepin and the beautiful Falls of St. Anthony excited his imagination. He speaks, also, of the cave still to be seen near St. Paul, at Dayton's Bluff.

" The Indians term it Wakan-tipi. The entrance is about ten feet wide, the height of it five feet. The arch within is fifteen feet high and about thirty feet broad; the bottom consists of fine, clear sand. About thirty feet from the entrance begins a lake, the water of which is transparent, and extends to an unsearchable distance, for the darkness of the cave prevents all attempts to acquire knowledge of it. I threw a small pebble towards the interior part of it with my utmost strength. I could hear that it fell into the water, and, notwithstanding it was of a small size, it caused an astonishing and terrible noise, that reverberated through those gloomy regions. I found in the cave many Indian hieroglyphics, which appeared very ancient, for time had nearly covered them with moss, so that it was with difficulty I could trace them. They were cut in a rude manner upon the inside of the wall, which was composed of a stone so extremely soft that it might be easily penetrated with a knife; a stone everywhere to be found near the Mississippi.

" At a little distance from this dreary cavern is the burial place of several bands of the Naudowessie Indians. Though these people have no fixed residence, being in tents, and seldom but a few months in one spot, yet they always bring the bones of the dead to this place."

At a funeral of a Sioux chief he was admitted to the council, but they would not permit a stranger to see their burial place. The Sioux braves, to show theii soiiow, pieiced theii aims with aiiows and the women gashed theii flesh with bioken flints.

Written in Caivei's book is a buiial oiation deliveied ovei a dead chief of the Dakotahs. Schillei, the gieat poet of the Geimans, at one time iead this oiation and wiote a poem, one of his veiy best, fiom Carvei's suggestions. The poem, " Song of the Nadouessioux Chief," is given heie, as tians- lated by Sii John Heischel:

SONG OF THE NADOUESSIOUX CHIEF.

See, wheie upon the mat he sits
    Eiect, befoie his dooi,
With just the same majestic aii
    That once in life he woie.

But wheie is fled his stiength of limb,
    The whiilwind of his bieath?
To the Gieat Spiiit, when he sent
    The peace pipe's mounting wieath.

Wheie are those falcon eyes, which late
    Along the plain could tiace,
Along the giass's dewy waves
    The reindeer's piinted pace?

Those legs, which once with matchless speed,
  Flew through the drifted snow,
Surpassed the stag's unwearied course,
  Outran the mountain roe?

Those arms, once used with might and main,
  The stubborn bow to twang.
See, see, their nerves are slack at last,
  All motionless they hang.

'T is well with him, for he has gone
  Where snow no more is found,
Where the gay thorn's perpetual bloom
  Decks all the field around.

Where wild birds sing from every spray,
  Where deer come sweeping by,
Where fish from every lake afford
  A plentiful supply.

With spirits now he feasts above,
  And leaves us here alone,
To celebrate his valiant deeds,
  And round his grave to mourn.

Sound the death song, bring forth the gifts,
  The last gifts of the dead —
Let all which may yield him joy
  Within his grave be laid.

The hatchet place beneath his head,
  Still red with hostile blood;
And add, because the way is long,
  The bear's fat limbs for food.

The scalping-knife beside him lay,
  With paints of gorgeous dye,
That in the land of souls his form
  May shine triumphantly.

Although the country was a thousand miles from any English settlement, the explorer felt certain the beauty and fertility of the country about the Minnesota would soon attract settlers. "And the future settlers," says he, "will be able to convey their produce most easily down to the Gulf of Mexico, the current of the Mississippi being favorable to small craft. In time," he adds, "canals might be cut and communication opened by water with New York by way of the lakes."

Carver went from Minnesota to England, and died there, very poor, in 1780.

VIEWS AT FORT SNELLING.

EARLY DAYS AT FORT SNELLING.

Enteied and occupied for the first time in the yeai 1821, by Colonel Snelling and the Fifth United States Infantry, Foit Snelling has stood eighty yeais. It was built in the shape of a lozenge at the junction of the Mississippi and Minnesota iiveis. The fiist baiiacks for the soldieis weie log cabins, but afteiwaids all the houses weie of stone. At the foit lived the wives and childien of the officeis, and one of the childien, now Mis. Chailotte Wisconsin Van Cleve, a resident of Minneapolis, tells what happened theie when she was a little giil:

"Indians veiy often came to the foit, painted and

on the war path against some neighboring tribe;
sometimes traders and cattle-men came, or the
French *coureur-de-bois*. One October day seven
Indian women came paddling down the great
'Father of Waters' in their canoes, and not seeing
the rapids soon enough, were drawn over the Falls
of St. Anthony into the foaming waters below and
would have lost their lives but for the help of the
brave soldier boys. In March of the next year
about three feet of snow fell and the poor Indians
suffered greatly.

"On one occasion thirty lodges of Sisseton Sioux
were caught in a terrible snow storm on a large
prairie. The storm lasted so long that many of the
Indians starved to death, and all might have died
but for a strong and courageous warrior, who
started off on snow shoes for the nearest trading
post, one hundred miles away, to bring help. Four
Canadians went back with him, carrying food to the
sufferers, and brought the remnant of the Indians to
the fort.

"The next yeai the Indians near the foit giew veiy angiy at the white men and threatened to do them harm. One June day, two boats were

OLD BLOCK HOUSE. FORT SNELLING,

coming up the Mississippi rivei with food for the soldiers at Foit Snelling. At Wapasha's village, wheie the city of Winona is now, the Dakotahs oideied the ciew to come ashoie. When the boat-men landed, howevei, and saw that the Indians meant to kill them, they wished to get away again,

for they had no guns, so the captain· assumed a
brave face and ordered the Indians to leave the
boats.   For a wonder they did — they were afraid of
the daring captain.   Before they started back the
men in the boats were all given muskets and a
barrel of cartridges.   It was well it was so, too.

"At the mouth of the Bad Axe River the savages
attacked the men in the boats, and from their canoes
tried to climb into the white man's vessel.   The
boatmen were getting safely away, when suddenly
their little craft stopped — it had run upon a sand
bar!   A young warrior mounted the deck and began
to fire his gun at the voyagers — they gave themselves up for lost.   But no!   One of the men,
'Saucy Jack' they call him, shoots the Indian, and
jumping into the water, begins pushing the boat
back into the channel; some of the others help, and
soon, although the bullets splash the water all about
them, they get safely away, all but two who had
fallen in the first fire of the Indians from their
ambush on the bank.

"The Chippewas and the Dakotahs have been mortal enemies as long as the oldest tribesmen can remember. The only name for the Dakotahs in the Chippewa language is Nadouessioux, which means 'enemies.' It is from the last syllable of this word that we get the name Sioux for this tribe. Many an exciting experience has come to the people at the fort caused by the incessant warring upon one another by bands from these tribes so hostile to each other. It is historic that a running fight between a handful of Dakotahs and a band of Chippewas took place in the streets of St. Paul as late as 1853."

THE FIRST STEAM-BOAT.

AN OLD TRAPPER'S STORY OF THE EARLY DAYS.

In those days there was a settlement just below St. Paul, called "Pig's Eye," and right across the river from it was Little Crow's village, Kaposia. A stalwart, strapping brave was this Little Crow; and his two sinewy sons, young bucks, quite like their father — "chips of the old block," indeed.

When Crow and I were younger, I chanced across him one day caught in a bear trap and helped him out. Well, there wasn't anything too good for me after that. If I happened along at his place on one of my trips, the freedom of his lodge was mine and all there was in it. Why, I have known him to stalk up and down the street of his village, all through a winter's night, with only a thin blanket over him, in order that I might have his lodge and furs to cover me. Yes, sir! And you couldn't refuse, save you offended. But his kind were as few and far between as the footprints of them on the warpath.

I think it was in the spring of 1823 I was out from Fort Snelling with a message for down the river. You see there were rumors of an outbreak of the reds, and Colonel Snelling wanted ammunition and re-enforcements from down below, and so asked me to carry the message, because any one else might have been suspected. On the way down I stopped at Little Crow's village for the night, thinking I might hear or see something to show me how the reds were feeling.

With his usual gravity the chief greeted me and led me to his lodge, where we sat ourselves down on the furs before the door. His squaw brought him his pipe of red sand-stone, with a stem of reed hung with gorgeously colored feathers, and with much solemnity the old chief lighted it with an ember from the lodge fire, smoked a few minutes in silence and then handed the pipe to me. Slowly I puffed at it, and blew the smoke up into the air in curls and rings. It was a long time before I handed the calumet back to him that he might knock the ashes out against the ground. Then it was he felt free to speak, gazing fixedly into the lodge fire.

"Little Crow is glad to see his white brother," said he.

"Little Crow is kind," I gravely responded, gazing also at the burning embers.

"Does my brother no more trap the beaver in the river, or hunt the deer in the forest, that Little Crow sees him so little of late?"

"The white man is getting too old and stiff to sleep in the woods, and stays with his brothers up yonder at the fort," said I, wondering while I spoke if he would believe me, yet not knowing what else to say.

"My brother should learn of the poor Indian, and

LITTLE CROW'S SON.

oil his muscles that they giow not stiff." His tone implied all I expected it to; I could not hope to deceive him; he did not expect the tiuth.

"And wheie does my biother ventuie now and alone?" he went on.

"Down the iivei to meet a gieat chief who comes to visit at the foit."

"My biothei did well to taiiy at Kaposia," finished Little Ciow, and he had me some suppei biought, spiead on the baik of tiees, and left me alone for the night.

This was not the fiist time I had slept among the Indians, as I have alieady told you, and I had always found them most hospitable and caieful of my wants. I do not doubt that if I had been Ciow's enemy instead of his fiiend, but what he would have tieated me as well while his guest.

At the faithei end of the village stieet I now noticed a tall heap, or beacon, of diy wood of some consideiable size, and being added to continually by the squaws. Even as I watched them, they stopped

their work and went about other business. This
pile of wood was for their council-fire, I surmised.
There would be a great pow-wow to-night, and I
had come just in time. For long enough I sat there
in front of the lodge after my meal, thinking over
the situation. If this council meant anything to us;
if it threatened the fort with attack, deeds would
follow hard upon words; but how to find out if the
council meant mischief, and then how to get the
news to Colonel Snelling? These were the
questions.

Meanwhile the huge pile had been lighted, and
the flames leaping upward in the darkness threw
their lurid light upon the warriors, who were beginning to assemble for the "big talk." I knew that
some time would elapse before the preliminary smok-
ing and the long silence that always precedes the
Indian discussion, were over and the talking began;
so I sat on, planning as to how I might hear the
harangues unseen and without being missed.

Finally, seeing that the attention of all was taken

up by the long-winded speech of a paiticulaily
vocifeious chief, and the women and childien being
gatheied close outside the ciicle of biaves, I ciept
unnoticed to a piotecting clump of willows within
eaishot of the loud-voiced councilloi, whom I
iecognized as Little Ciow himself. The shadowy
silhouette of the savage looked giotesque enough
in the semi-daikness about the fire — a veiitable
jumping-jack — his head-diess of featheis swaying this way and that, and his long aims flying
about like the vanes of a wind-mill. So much I
noticed befoie the sense of what he was saying
came to me.

" When last the voice of the Gieat Spiiit spoke to
us, uiging that we no longei submit to the wiongs
the white man has inflicted upon us; uiging that we
be no moie a cowaid iace, but dig up the ied tomahawk, and put on again the featheis and wai paint
of othei days when we weie not so laggaid in
prepaiation for battle; swift messengeis ian fiom
village to village and soon the war parties began to

assemble; in the night was heard the call of the
screech owl, by day the call of the crow and the cat-
bird, and many chiefs with their young men were
here ready for the fray.   Then why sit we here now
and fear the attempt ?   Are we all grown cowards
and afraid of death?

" Is the scare we got at that time still with you?
Wahpeton says the terrible beast we saw in the
river on the day of the attack was sent to devour
us; that it was not the voice of the Great Spirit our
medicine men had heard, but the words of an Evil
Spirit, who meant that we should be destroyed;
that the Great Spirit was angry and sent the smok-
ing canoe against us.   We were cowards then, and
ran away back to our villages, and the white men at
the fort were saved that time.   But we know how
false are Wahpeton's words: the great canoe that
smokes and shrieks we have seen many times since,
and know it is but the magic of the white man and
cannot harm us."

So this was the reason, thought I, why the attack

which had threatened the fort some months since was put off. The first steamer which ascended the river to St. Paul had scared off the reds.

But Little Crow was still exhorting his braves, and finally he won them to his way of thinking, and the attack was settled to begin in three days, or as soon as the warriors from the other village could be assembled.

I had learned what I came for and crept back silently to the lodge. To my surprise I found the remains of my supper, which I had left on the ground where I had sat, were gone and the fire had been replenished. Did they know I had crept off, or had they supposed me sleeping in the lodge? Knowing my destination, and that I could not return in time to warn the fort, they might well be unconcerned as to what I found out. Assuredly, however, they would never let me carry the news I had heard to Fort Snelling. But might I not send it?

We had at times amused Little Crow, when at the

foit, by wiiting his name on his thumb-nail and sending him to some of the officeis to have them iead it. It used to tickle the chief immensely to heai each one iead the same thing fiom his nail, and he many times had pionounced it " magic." Could I get him to go to the foit now?

In the moining Little Ciow came to see me, his squaws with him biinging my bieakfast, and inquiied if I was to stait immediately. Upon my answeiing " Yes," he said a paity of his young men weie going on a hunting tiip in theii canoes a few miles down the iivei, and he would have them wait for me. So! I was to be pievented fiom going anywheie but down the iivei!

Just befoie staiting, I ventuied to put my plan to the test. Colonel Snelling, I told the chief, had wished me to stop on my way down and ask Little Ciow to visit him to-day, as he had fiiends with him who wished to see the gieat Indian chief. The scheme worked! Ciow giavely said he would go immediately. Was he thinking of looking the foit over to get a better knowledge of it, preparatory to the attack? Should I prick his name upon his thumb? I asked. When he unsuspectingly reached me his hand, I scratched, "Hold him," deep into the nail and colored it black.

Well, he went, as he said he would, and upon one pretence or another they held him for weeks at the fort, until the scare was over and the warriors had gone back home. The reds would not, as I surmised, attack without their leader, and Little Crow would find it hard to explain his absence when next he wanted his braves to fight.

CAN-KU WAS-TE WIN.

THE SIOUX AND THEIR WAYS.

The Chippewa Indians of the Lake Superior region call their enemies in their own language, "Nadouessioux"; this name they applied especially to their greatest foes, the Dakotahs, and it was often used, after the white man came to the Northwest, by the traders in speaking of the Dakotahs. The word was shortened by them to Sioux, but we must remember that that name is not the proper one; Dakotah is the only name the Indian knows himself by.

"The Sioux," says one of our historians, who has lived long among them, "live in tepees, or circular, conical tents, supported by poles, so arranged as to leave an opening in the top for ventilation and for the escape of smoke. These were, before the advent of the whites, covered with dressed buffalo

53

skins, but more recently with a coarse cotton tent cloth, which is preferable on account of its being much lighter to transport from place to place, as being almost constantly on the move, the tents being carried by the squaws.

"There is no more comfortable habitation than the Sioux tepee to be found among the dwellers in tents anywhere. A fire is made in the center for either warmth or cooking purposes. The camp kettle is suspended over it, making cooking easy and cleanly. In the winter, when the Indian family settles down to remain any considerable time, they select a river bottom where there is timber or chaparral, and set up the tepee; then they cut the long grass or bottom cane, and stand it up against the outside of the lodge to the thickness of about twenty inches, and you have a very warm and cosy habitation.

" The wealth of the Sioux consists very largely in his horses, and his subsistence is the game of the forest and plains and the fish and wild rice of the lakes. Minnesota was an Indian paradise. It abounded in buffalo, elk, moose, deer, beaver, wolves, and, in fact, nearly all wild animals found in North America. It held upon its surface eight thousand beautiful lakes, alive with the finest edible fish. It was dotted over with beautiful groves of the sugar maple, yielding quantities of delicious sugar, and wild rice swamps were abundant. An inhabitant of this region, with absolute liberty, and nothing to do but defend it against the encroachments of enemies, certainly had very little more to ask of his Creator. But he was not allowed to enjoy it in peace. A stronger race was on his trail, and there was nothing left for him to do but surrender his country on the best terms he could make."

W. H. Keating, who was the scientist with Major Long's expedition, which arrived at Lake Traverse in July, 1823, thus speaks of Wanatan, the most distinguished chief of the Yankton tribe of Sioux:

"In the summer of 1822, he undertook a journey, from which, apprehending much danger on the part of the Chippewas, he made a vow to the sun that if he returned safe he would abstain from all food or drink for the space of four successive days and nights, and that he would distribute among his people all the property which he possessed, including his lodges, horses and dogs. On his return, which happened without accident, he celebrated the dance of the Sun. This consisted in making three cuts through his skin, one on his breast and one on each of his arms. The skin was cut in the manner of a loop, so as to permit a rope to pass under the strip of skin and flesh which was thus divided from the body. The ropes being passed through, their ends were secured to a tall, vertical pole, planted at about forty yards from his lodge. He then began to dance around the pole, at the commencement of his fast, frequently swinging himself in the air, so as to be supported merely by the cords which were secured to the strips of skin cut off from his arms and breast.

"He continued this exercise, with few intermissions, during the whole of his fast, until the fourth day, about ten o'clock A. M., when the strip of skin from his breast gave way. Notwithstanding which he interrupted not his dance, although merely supported by his arms. At noon the strip from his left arm snapped off. His uncle then thought he had suffered enough; he drew his knife and cut off the skin of his right arm, upon which Wanatan fell to the ground and swooned. The heat at this time was extreme. He was left exposed to the sun until night, when his friends brought him some provisions. After the ceremony was over he distributed to them his property, among which were five fine horses, and he and his two squaws left his lodge, abandoning every article of their furniture."

The Indians were not at all choice in their eating. The same writer as above tells of the feast of buffalo stew and *dog meat*, dressed without salt, which was set before him and his fellows; the latter he says, was very fat, sweet and palatable.

THE RANGERS OF THE FOREST.

As furs grew more and more scarce within easy reach of Quebec and Montreal, the Indians were persuaded to go farther and farther into the forest after them. Along with the Indians went adventurous Frenchmen, learning where the best hunting and trapping grounds lay. Thus the trade in furs grew, and from far distant Ouisconsin and the banks of the Minnesota, "the sky-tinted water," were brought the pelts of the beaver and mink. Once a year the tribes bordering on the great lakes — Chippewas from Lake Superior and Winnebagos from Lake Michigan — came paddling down in their canoes, now loaded with skins, to Michilimackinac, to return laden with powder and bright hatchets.

From this trade there sprang up a new class of

men, the *coureurs de bois*. In the beginning these were the men who had accompanied the Indians on their hunting trips and who had made themselves well acquainted with the paths and places of the fur-bearing animals of the woods; these now became, however, the middle men and peddlers of the trade. Loading their canoes at Michilimackinac with bright colored cloths, blankets, beads, axes, knives, arms and ammunition, early some bright sunshiny morning they pushed off into the steaming Lake Michigan, paddled up Green River and down the Ouisconsin into the great " Father of Waters"; thence, perhaps up the Minnesota, trading along the way; sometimes they stopped for months among the Indians, even marrying Indian wives.

" Twelve, fifteen, eighteen months would often elapse without any tidings of them, when they would come sweeping their way down the lake in full glee, their canoes laden down with packs of beaver skins. Now came their turn for revelry and extravagance. ' You would be amazed,' says an old writer, ' if you saw how lavish these peddlers are when they return; how they feast and game, and how prodigal they are, not only in their clothes, but upon their sweethearts. Such of them as are married have the wisdom to retire to their own houses; but the bachelors act just as an East Indiaman and pirates are wont to do; for they lavish, eat, drink, and play all the way as long as the goods hold out; and when these are gone, they even sell their embroidery, their lace, and their clothes. This done, they are forced upon a new voyage for subsistence!'

" Many of these *coureurs de bois* became so accustomed to the Indian mode of living, and the perfect freedom of the wilderness, that they lost all relish for civilization, and identified themselves with the savages among whom they dwelt. Their conduct and example gradually corrupted the natives, and impeded the works of the Catholic missionaries, who were at this time prosecuting their pious labors in the wilds of Canada.

" To check these abuses, and to protect the fur

tiade fiom various iiiegulaiities piacticed by these loose adventuieis, an oidei was issued by the Fiench Goveinment piohibiting all persons, on pain of death, fiom tiading into the inteiioi of the countiy without a license."

Things weie, howevei, soon as bad as befoie — the peison to whom the license was given sending out fiom six to ten of the iangeis — and although the pious missionaiies laboied haid to conveit the Indians, theii woik was often counteiacted by these "ienegades fiom civilization!"

Lax as these iangers weie, peihaps, in theii moials, we must not foiget that it was in theii wake that civilization spiead and the pioneei maiched. To them is due, in gieat pait, the eaily opening of the West to settlement. Settlement would have been much more difficult without the *coureurs de bois* to blaze the way for the pioneei.

OLD STATE CAPITOL OF MINNESOTA.

THE DRUM-BEAT OF THE MINNESOTA FIRST.

"Ma, have you read the *Press?*"

"I? What time have I to see the papers? No, of course not. Why? More news about that robber?"

"No, that isn't it. But those secesh fellows have gone and fired on that fort in Charleston Harbor, because General Anderson wouldn't surrender."

"No; you can't mean it! And what did Anderson do?"

"Oh, he didn't surrender, not he! Say, yes — he — did — too. It goes on to say that 'finally he saw he could hold out no longer, so he surrendered, and Beauregarde allowed him to march out of the fort with colors flying and the men carrying their arms.' Well, say! Surrendered!"

Such was the conversation that took place in a

little cottage in St. Paul, the capital of our baby state of Minnesota, Monday evening, April 15, 1861. Hardly had Mr. Pierson finished speaking, when the door quickly opened and in rushed sixteen-year-old Harry, wild-eyed and tumble-headed, crying, "The North's gone to war with the South, pa! Governor Ramsey's telegraphed home from Washington; says he's offered a regiment to Mr. Lincoln and it has been accepted, and for the lieutenant-governor to call right off for volunteers!"

"Where did you hear all that, son?"

"Down to the hotel, ma; everybody's talking about it down there, and they say that Governor Ramsey went to the war-office first thing yesterday morning and told Secretary Cameron he had a thousand men ready to go at any time; so Minnesota has made the first offer of soldiers to defend the Government. Pa, can't I go?"

"Where to?"

"Go to war, pa. You know the Pioneer Guards have just had a meeting at the armory, and lots of men signed a paper volunteering to go. Mr. King, over on the next street, was the first to sign his name, and that makes him the first man in the whole United States to volunteer for the war. Pa, let me sign."

" You are too young, Harry; they wouldn't take you."

" If they take me, pa, can I go? "

" Yes, if they will take you."

Mr. Pierson thought the question settled, for he felt very sure a boy as young as Harry would not be wanted.

In the morning came Acting-Governor Ignatius Donnelly's call for volunteers — for one regiment of ten companies — and so quickly and enthusiastically was it answered that by the 29th of April, the ten desired companies were all assembled at Fort Snelling. Public meetings had been held in all the larger towns, addressed by prominent men of both the great political parties, urging the people to rally to the support of the flag; and the feeling of the people of

NEW STATE CAPITOL OF MINNESOTA.

Minnesota was manifest by the number of volunteers offering themselves for service; so many more than were needed, that a second regiment was soon started. The militia organizations volunteering were the St. Paul, Faribault, Winona, Dakotah, Wabasha and Goodhue Volunteers, the Pioneer, Stillwater and Lincoln Guards, and the St. Anthony Zouaves.

Nothing more was heard from Harry about enlisting for two weeks, when, coming in to dinner on Monday, he quietly said, " Well, pa, I've enlisted."

" You — have — what ! "

" I was seventeen yesterday, pa, and I went over to Fort Snelling and told the captain you said I might enlist if he'd take me, and he — he — took me, pa."

" Well, I say ! "

" And it was just grand, pa; they ran up the colors at the old flag-staff, and the cannon fired thirty-four shots, one for every state, and they had a big dinner spread out on a board table, with a tin plate and cup for every soldier. They had the barracks all scrubbed out and clean straw put on the floor, and we will sleep there until orders come to go to Washington, and —"

There was no need to ask what Harry's feelings were on the question. He was wildly excited; the seriousness of his undertaking had not yet occurred to him, nor would it, probably, until home had been left far behind, and actual camp duties had been begun.

Mrs. Pierson had quietly left the room in tears. She knew no word of hers could alter the case in any way now; and her heart ached at the thought of losing her only child, perhaps never to see him again. Poor mothers! How much they have sacrificed for the cause of progress! That nations might prosper and civilization grow, they have given up all they hold the dearest since ever time began. Bless the mothers!

So it was settled that Harry should go with the regiment when it went out from the state to fight its country's battles in the South. And we find him one Saturday morning in the latter part of June, embarking on the steamer *War Eagle*, at Fort Snelling. The *War Eagle* and the *Northern Belle* landed the whole regiment, at an early hour, at the upper levee in St. Paul, where the boys marched across the city to the lower levee, and there going aboard the steamers, again sailed away down the river for Prairie du Chien and La Crosse. Harry had seen his parents as the regiment went through St. Paul, but had time only to kiss his hand to his mother and wave a last good-bye as they marched past.

On the way down the river, there were crowds gathered on the levees to cheer the boys in blue as they passed down, and at three o'clock in the morning, when the boat tied up at the wharf in Prairie du Chien, the whole of the inhabitants of the town were there to meet it, firing cannons and cheering lustily. The railroad furnished its best cars to carry the Minnesota boys, and gave them a bountiful dinner on the way.

Through Chicago, where speeches were made by

the mayor and others, through Fort Wayne, Ind., and Pittsburgh, Penn., they rode, to Harrisburg, where they camped for a day, waiting for instructions. At Huntingdon, Penn., a little village in the mountains, the boys were pleasantly surprised by the ladies of the place, who brought in sandwiches, doughnuts and delicious coffee. All the journey to Harrisburg, indeed, was a continuous ovation, but at that city they began to experience more of the serious side of a soldier's life, for here a train of cattle cars was backed upon the siding and the soldiers called upon to clamber aboard.

"Quite a change, is n't it, Harry?" called out one of Harry's tent-mates, as they stood in company awaiting their turn.

"Surely they don't intend us to travel to Washington in those things, do they, Brown?"

"Looks that way, Harry."

"Why, what will we sit on?"

"On your thumb, I guess, my boy; I don't see anything else unless you use your knapsack."

"Such ill-smelling things are not fit to carry hogs in."

"Right you are, Harry, but what are you going to do? Cheer up, all things go with the trade;" and Brown laughed gayly as he helped his young comrade into the car and climbed in himself.

The first indications of war came from a woman, as the train hurried by a beautiful country home; she stood on the veranda spitefully shaking a broom at the soldiers in the cars, who cheered and waved their hats in return. The next evidence of hostility was in Baltimore where, on the nineteenth of April, the Sixth Massachusetts regiment had been stoned and three of its members killed by a mob. The same crowd stood scowlingly waiting to receive the Minnesota boys, but a display of bayonets kept them at a distance.

Late in the afternoon other cars of a little better kind were taken for Washington, which Harry and his comrades reached about ten o'clock in the evening. After some delay shelter was found for the tired troops in the assembly rooms, and not many minutes afterward Colonel Aldrich arrived at the quarters, followed by a whole squad of colored servants with pails of coffee, huge baskets of sandwiches, and relays of pies, cakes and doughnuts; and never had food tasted better. Mr. Aldrich was a Member of Congress from Minnesota and a very open-handed, generous man, who had many times during the war proved himself the friend of the soldier, and especially of the Minnesota boys.

Early the following morning, Harry felt someone shaking him, and waked up enough to find Brown standing over him and to hear that young fellow say:

"Wake up! You'll be left. The regiment is on the march."

"Where are we going now?"

"Don't know. Are you awake?"

Harry said he thought he was, and rolled out of his blanket to find most of his companions gone, only a few of the younger ones, tired out like himself, being still in the assembly chamber. Hurrying out with these, he found the regiment forming in front of the Capitol, each man wondering what the matter was and hoping the rebels had attacked Washington, as was rumored; but war was not to commence for them for some days yet.

Harry soon found they were only going into camp for awhile on a rising piece of ground just east of the Capitol about a mile. Here they stayed drilling and marching, marching and drilling, until July 3, spending the time when not on duty in examining the public buildings, the only objects of interest in the whole city; for Washington was not then the "City of Magnificent Distances."

The streets of Washington in 1861 were unpaved and in wet weather the heavy army wagons were often mired in Pennsylvania Avenue. The old canal reeked with malarious and foul smells. The dome of the Capitol and the senate wing were unfinished, and most of the shops and residences were old, dilapidated and neglected in appearance. A few years afterward all this was changed and

Washington became the most beautiful city in the whole United States.

Our young soldier boy had by this time become most popular among his companions because of his cheerful temper and happy disposition, and his comrades took care that time did not lie heavy upon his hands. So whatever excursion or pleasure party was planned he was always invited; he did not become homesick, therefore, with so much to take up his attention.

Hard-tack and salt pork do not make the best kind of fare. The hard-tack had the letters "B. C." marked upon it, and Brown suggested one day at mess that perhaps the letters stood for the date of the baking; the pork was good, excellent,—so those reported who had good teeth and strong jaws. What wonder foraging was resorted to, even though forbidden by camp rules.

One day Harry and young Brown, with a few others from the same tent, were returning to camp, bringing the dressed quarters of a young beef. It was rather risky work and swift punishment generally followed the apprehension of any such delinquent. When nearly to the camp one of the men sung out, as a number of officers came around a bend in the road:

" There's Colonel Franklin ahead."

" What shall we do now, run?" asked another.

"Can't do anything but face the music, can we?" replied Harry.

And the officer having seen the culprits, it did seem useless to run. Harry was appointed spokesman for them all and had made up his mind to tell the truth in answer to Colonel Franklin's questions, when Colonel Gorman, of the Minnesota regiment, who happened to be mounted, rode up and began to denounce his soldiers, breaking off in the midst to request Colonel Franklin to leave the men to him for such punishment as would be an effective example to the regiment.

Colonel Franklin walked away, and Gorman, turning to the offenders, said:

"Now, take up that beef and go to your regiment, and don't disgrace it by ever getting *caught* in any such scrape again."

And you may be sure they never did.

The Minnesota regiment was next sent to Alexandria, Va., to go into camp, and it was from here they were ordered to Manassas Junction, where the enemy was in force and where, in the Battle of Bull Run, Harry first smelled the smoke of battle and became acquainted with the horrors of war.

While his company was hurrying over one part of the battle field, Harry dropped out of the ranks to say a few words to a poor, wounded comrade, who was crying out at the cruelty of his companions in leaving him to the rebels. He quieted the wounded man; then as he had seen the flag of a field hospital flying in a grove near by, picked the fellow up, and staggering under his weight, carried him toward the woods.

Just then a platoon of the enemy wheeled out of another clump of woods opposite, and hurried across

the open towards our young soldier. Evidently
they were marching to that quarter of the battle-
field from which the noise of the firing came.
Harry dropped the wounded man — not wishing to
be taken prisoner — and bounded away towards a
near by ravine, reaching it just in time to hear the
" chug " of the muskets as they fell forward into the
left hands of the rebels. He threw himself down
the bank of the ravine and the bullets whizzed harm-
lessly over his head.

He sprang up and, glancing back, saw a row
of blank faces, astonished at seeing him break
down the ravine out of range. Reaching the wood
he hid until the platoon had passed by; then making his way back to the wounded man, carried him
safely to the hospital. After seeing him in the
hands of the surgeon, Harry hastened to rejoin his
regiment.

Many times on that terrible July day did Minnesota have reason to be proud of her boys. Bull
Run might well have been won three times over had

all fought as well as they. Nor in that terrible
retreat to Centerville have we less reason to feel
proud. Colonel Gorman offered his regiment as
rear guard and was assigned next to that position,
the Minnesota First marching off down the road in
perfect order, in strong contrast to other disordered
mobs of fleeing soldiery.

Going through Centerville, the regiment halted,
and Harry, tired and worn out, dropped upon the
ground where he was and fell asleep immediately.
In about half an hour, however, he was aroused and
called up for coffee, after which the march was again
taken up for Alexandria.

This was the hardest of all. They knew they had
met with a repulse, but had not realized that it was
to be accepted as defeat, and there was some
grumbling heard in the ranks. Again, the prospect
of a tramp of twenty-five miles, after such a day of
phenomenal heat, long marches and hard fighting,
seemed an impossible undertaking. How he did it,
Harry could not have told afterwards.

Loaded down with knapsack, haversack, musket, and forty rounds of cartridges, several times during the night he was awakened from deep sleep by stumbling against a stone or other obstruction. Brown offered to help him, but Harry refused.

"I will march till I drop, Brown, before I'll give in or let any one help me," said he; but it was easy to see at what cost he was keeping up: his set, drawn face, shuffling, mechanical step, and staggering gait told its own story.

In the forenoon of the next day, he was back in his tent at Alexandria, thoroughly exhausted, and was soon asleep. But in the afternoon the soldiers were once more called up and marched to Washington in a heavy rain, and then, cold and wet, kept standing on the street for an hour, until quarters could be provided.

The regiment later went into camp a short distance east of the Capitol and resumed daily drills. Deaths and captures had caused a number of vacancies in the regiment, and many promotions and appointments were made to fill them, new names being posted daily.

Brown, who was now in the same mess as Harry, came running into the tent one day with his face full of news.

"You have been posted, Harry," he cried.

"For what ?"

"I don't know for what ; perhaps for carrying that wounded fellow into the hospital.   At least, you are among those promoted."

"To what, Brown?"

"Lieutenant."

Here others hurried up and began to shake Harry by the hand and congratulate him on his good luck.

So it was as company lieutenant that our youthful Minnesotan served his country during the rest of the summer of '61, and until September, 1862, at Antietam, when he was wounded in the thigh and confined for some weeks to the hospital. Being granted a furlough until such time as he was able once more to march with his comrades, he spent the winter of '62 and '63 in New York, visiting his cousins. His father and mother came on from the West to see their son. They spent a month with him, and altogether the winter was a most enjoyable one.

Reporting for duty early in the year, he was again assigned to his old regiment as captain of Company H; not the company, you will remember, of his enlistment. Many of his old comrades met him upon his return, but others who had fallen in battle were not there to greet him; altogether the whole regiment contained but two hundred and sixty-two men.

The great battle at Gettysburg was the first important engagement Harry was in after his return, and it was here that the First Minnesota won its fame. As the battle of Gettysburg was the turning point of the Civil War, so was the fight made by the Minnesotans the turning point of that battle. The stand taken that day by the boys from the Gopher State won the battle of Gettysburg, and turned the

tide of the war in favor of the North. All honor to
the Minnesota First! "The Spartans did not inquire
how many the enemy are, but where they are."

A considerable portion of the Third Army Corps,
under General Sickles, in full retreat from the
Confederates, had passed the Minnesota regiment.
Harry and his comrades now numbering, as we have
said, only two hundred and sixty-two officers and
men, stood, awaiting orders, on the brow of a slope,
as General Hancock rode up and tried in vain to
stop the fleeing soldiers. Reinforcements were coming, but what to do to hold the position until they
arrived!

"What regiment is this?" cried Hancock, riding
to where stood the boys from the Northwest.

"First Minnesota," came the answer.

"Charge those lines!" commanded the general.

The charge was ordered and gallantly made.
That mere handful of brave Minnesotans charged
the long lines of well-ordered graycoats, held them
until the reserves came up, and saved the day!

" The Spartans did not inquire how many the enemy are, but where they are."

This was the last battle of importance that Harry was in. Early in the following year orders were received for the regiment to return to Minnesota. Leaving the railroad at La Crosse, the soldier boys were bundled into sleighs and driven on the frozen Mississippi to Fort Snelling, where the final muster-out came.

The welcome home given our young captain by his friends and schoolmates may well be left to the imagination. Suffice it to say that two hearts at least were made glad as Harry's father and mother received him safely returned to them once more.

KISH-KAH-NAH-CUT.

THE OUTBREAK OF THE SIOUX.
1862.

In the year 1862, the United States being at war, and large numbers of men having been sent out of the state to fill quotas in Minnesota regiments in the South, the Sioux Indians, both Upper and Lower Bands, decided that the time was ripe to kill all the whites and regain their old hunting grounds.

The Agency of the Upper Sioux was established at Yellow Medicine and that of the Lower Sioux at Redwood, both places being on the Minnesota River.

Some ten years before this, the Indians had made a treaty with the government, ceding certain of their lands to the United States. For the lands we were to pay the Indians a large sum of money every year, and the Indians were accustomed to come into the agency at stated periods to receive this money, their annuities.

The fact that in August, 1862, the money long due had not been paid, may have angered the Indians and turned their hands to bloodshed.

The first blood was shed at Acton. A few Indians had quarreled with a settler at that place about some eggs they wanted. One of the Indians, dared by the others, killed the white man, and then the whole family was murdered. Other Indians waiting at the agency for their annuities joined the murderers, and set upon the whites at Yellow Medicine with tomahawk, knife, and gun, putting them all to death. After this, the cruel red men separated into small squads of from five to ten, and spread over the country in every direction to the lonely homes of the settlers. One thousand pioneers, most of them defenseless women and little children, were coldly and cruelly murdered by the ruthless Sioux.

In attacking the isolated home of the farmer, this

was the method of attack: the party of Indians would call at the house, to ask for food or a drink of milk, and, being well known, would cause no alarm. Then they would await a good opportunity, and when the man was turned away from them, would treacherously shoot him in the back. Not even the poor mother was spared, though pleading with the savages to spare her and her little ones.

The Indians, having plundered and looted the house, carried off all that seemed valuable to them, burned the buildings and hurried off to the next farm to repeat the outrage. Occasionally some one would escape and spread the news of the massacre to the neighbors; then would follow a hurried packing of clothing and bedding, a bundling of food and children into wagons and a hurried flight to Fort Ridgely or other place of refuge.

MAJ. T. J. SHEHAN.
(Defender of Fort Ridgely)

CAPTAIN MARSH.

The report of the outbreak on the 18th of August had reached Fort Ridgely at 9 P. M. of the same day. Capt. John S. Marsh immediately despatched a courier after a company of soldiers which had left the fort early in the morning, under Lieutenant Sheehan, to go to Fort Ripley on the Upper Mississippi. Another detachment of about fifty, who were on their way to Fort Snelling, were hurriedly called back. Company B, Fifth Minnesota Volunteers, eighty men, were the only soldiers then at the fort.

Without waiting for the troops he had sent for to come in, Captain Marsh set out, with but half a hundred men and an interpreter, to punish the Indians. He started for the Redwood Agency, about twelve miles up the Minnesota, marching along the north bank towards Martell's Ferry. At

this place Captain Marsh intended to cross the river
and from there march up the south bank to the
Agency.

Four miles below this point, the ferryman met the
soldiers and told them that the Indians were everywhere killing and burning, and that the best thing
they could do was to hurry back to the fort.

The gallant captain hesitated not a moment.
"Forward!" he shouted. "We are here to protect
and defend the frontier, and do it we will, or die
doing it," and he hurried his soldiers onward.
Lying by the roadside, asleep in death, were many
of the settlers, mutilated and scalped; yet there was
no staying the little band of soldiers: they marched
on, even to certain death.

Near the ferry the company halts and a man is
sent forward to examine the ferry and see if all is
right. He soon returns and reports the way clear.
A solitary Indian warrior, mounted and painted,
now appears on the opposite bank and silently
beckons the soldiers across. Then he speaks to the

interpreter: "Come over; it is all right here," he says.

Captain Marsh wonders if the Indian who seems so friendly is not hoping the soldiers will cross, and then he and his Indian brothers can fire at the troops while crowded together on the ferry-boat. The captain is suspicious and orders his men not to stir from where they are until he can make sure none of their red foes are hidden in the wooded ravines across the river. Even while he views the opposite shore through his glass, and the men are quietly drinking water brought from the river, on every side sounds the dreaded war whoop. Indians, hundreds of them, rise out of the grass and brush all around them and begin to shoot down the devoted band.

Pierced by twenty balls, the aged interpreter falls from his saddle, and with him many more. What hope is there for this little handful of fighters, brave though they be, against so great odds? Yet steadily they fight their way back, down the river, as cool as if on parade duty; fight their way inch by inch, taking advantage of every tree and stump. Suddenly shots come from the rear. More Indians there! They have crossed the stream, and, taking advantage of a bend in its course, now have the soldiers at a double disadvantage. How escape now? To cut their way through this horde of savages is impossible! The only hope is in taking to the water and swimming to the other shore; no Indians are on that side.

Captain Marsh gave the order to cross. If the river was fordable, he thought, so much the better; but the river, anyway. Taking his sword in one hand and his revolver in the other he himself led the way, wading out into the stream. They soon saw they must swim, and those who could, struck out for the other shore; those who could not do so, remained hidden in the grass as best they could until nightfall, making their escape then under cover of darkness. The swimmers had almost reached the farther shore, when Captain Marsh, struck by a bullet, sank below the surface. The Indians, knowing he was an officer, did their utmost to kill him, and for weeks after the battle, they hung around the spot searching for his body, that they might get the scalp.

Thirteen reached the bank safely and returned to the fort that night. Those who had hidden in the brush made their way also to the fort or settlements, some who were badly wounded having to stay out two or three days.

Later the body of the captain was found by a searching party from the fort, and laid to rest by his sorrowing comrades in the military burying-ground at Fort Ridgely.

SERGEANT JONES AND THE THIRD OF AUGUST.

(By Quinn the Interpreter.)

I was looking towards the Agency and saw a large body of men coming in the direction of the fort (Fort Ridgely) and supposed them soldiers returning from the payment at Yellow Medicine. On a second look, I observed that they were mounted, and knowing this time that they must be Indians, was surprised at seeing a large body, as they were not expected. I resolved to go into the garrison to see what it meant, having at the time, not the least suspicion that the Indians intended any hostile demonstration.

When I arrived at the garrison, I found Sergeant Jones at the entrance with a mounted howitzer, charged with shell and canister-shot, pointed toward the Indians, who were removed but a short

94

distance fiom the guaid-house. I asked the sergeant if any dangei was appiehended.

" No," he ieplied indiffeiently, " but I think it a
good iule to obseive that a soldiei should always
be ready for any emeigency."

These Indians had iequested the piivilege to
dance in the inclosuie suiiounding the foit. On
this occasion that iequest was iefused them. But I
saw that about sixty yaids west of the guaid-house
the Indians weie making the necessaiy piepaiations
for a dance. I thought nothing of it, as they had
fiequently done the same thing, but a little farthei
iemoved fiom the foit, undei somewhat diffeient
ciicumstances. I consideied it a singulai exhibition
of Indian foolishness, and at the solicitation of a few
ladies, went out and was myself a spectatoi to the
dance.

When the dance was concluded, the Indians
sought and obtained peimission to encamp on some
iising giound about a quaitei of a mile west of the
gaiiison. To this giound they soon iepaiied, and

encamped for the night. The next morning, by ten o'clock, all had left the vicinity of the garrison, departing in the direction of the Lower Agency. This whole matter of the dance was so conducted as to lead most, if not all, the residents of the garrison to believe that the Indians had paid them that visit for the purpose of dancing and obtaining provisions for a feast.

Some things were observable that were unusual. The visitors were all warriors, ninety-six in number, all in undress, except a very few who wore calico shirts; in addition to this, they all carried arms, guns and tomahawks, with ammunition pouches suspended around their shoulders.

Previous to the dance, the war implements were deposited some two hundred yards distant, where they had left their ponies. But even this circumstance excited no suspicion of danger or hostilities in the minds of residents of the garrison. These residents were thirty-five men — thirty soldiers and five citizens — with a few women and children.

The guard that day consisted of three soldiers: one was walking leisurely to and fro in front of the guard-house; the other two were off duty, passing about and taking their rest; and all entirely without apprehension of danger from Indians or any other foe.

As the Indians left the garrison without doing any mischief, most of us supposed that no evil was meditated by them. But there was one man who acted on the supposition that there was always danger surrounding a garrison when visited by savages; that man was Sergeant Jones. From the time he took his position at the gun he never left it, but acted as he said he believed it best to do — to be always ready. He not only remained at the gun himself, but retained two other men, whom he had previously trained as assistants, to work the piece.

Shortly before dark, without disclosing his intentions, Sergeant Jones said to his wife: "I have a little business to attend to to-night; at bed-time I wish you to retire and not wait for me." As he had frequently done this before to discharge some official duty at the quartermaster's office, she thought it not singular, but did as he requested and retired at the usual hour. On awakening in the morning, she was surprised to find he was not there, and had not been in bed. In truth, this faithful soldier had stood by his gun throughout the entire night, ready to fire, if occasion required, at any moment during that time; nor could he be persuaded to leave that gun until all this party of Indians had entirely disappeared from the vicinity of the garrison.

Some two weeks after this time, these same Indians, with others, attacked Fort Ridgely and, after some ten days' siege, the garrison was relieved by the arrival of soldiers under Col. H. H. Sibley. The second day after Colonel Sibley arrived, a Frenchman of pure or mixed blood, appeared before Sergeant Jones in a very agitated manner, and intimated that he had some disclosures to make to him; the man, however, seemed so completely under the dominion of fear, that he was unable to divulge the great secret. " Why," said he, " they would kill me; they would kill my wife and children." Saying which he turned and walked away.

Shortly after the first interview, this man returned to Sergeant Jones, and again the sergeant urged him to disclose what he knew, promising him that if he would do so, he would keep his name a profound secret forever. Being thus assured, the Frenchman soon became more calm. Hesitating a moment, he inquired of Sergeant Jones if he remembered that some two weeks before a party of Indians came down to the fort to have a dance? Sergeant Jones replied that he did.

" Well," said the Frenchman, " do you know that these Indians were all warriors of Little Crow, or some of the other lower bands? Sir, these Indians had all been selected for the purpose, and came down to Fort Ridgely by the express command of Little Crow and the other chiefs, to get permission to dance; and when all suspicion should be completely lulled, in the midst of the dance, to seize their weapons, kill every person in the fort, capture the big guns, open the magazine, and secure the ammunition, when they were to be. joined by all the remaining warriors of the lower bands. Thus armed and increased by numbers they were to proceed together down the valley of the Minnesota. With this force and these weapons they were assured they could drive every white man beyond the Mississippi."

All this, the Frenchman informed Jones, he had learned by being present at a council, and from conversations had with other Indians, who had told him that they had gone to the garrison for that very purpose. When he had concluded this revelation, Sergeant Jones inquired, "Why did they not execute their purpose? Why did they not take the fort?"

"Because," answered the Frenchman, "during their dance and their whole stay at the fort, they saw that big gun constantly pointed at them."

THE ATTACK ON FORT RIDGELY.

August 20 and 22.

Foit Ridgely, on the Minnesota, baiied the way of the Indians to New Ulm and St. Petei, and must be destioyed. Two attacks weie accoidingly made, one on the 20th of August and the othei two days afteiwaids.

Ridgely was a foit only in name, being but a gioup of log and fiame buildings, with a baiiacks of stone, aiianged in the foim of a squaie. It stood on a spui of the praiiie tableland, oveilooking the Minnesota Rivei to the south, and flanked on the east and west by deep iavines. Both by construction and location it was difficult of defense.

Without waining of any kind, the savages attacked the foit fiom the iavine on the east eaily in the afteinoon. By quick woik on the pait of the gunneis, Whipple, McGrew, and Jones, and the able defense of these guns by the infantiy, the post was saved, not until, howevei, the Indians had succeeded in stampeding the goveinment mules and officeis' hoises. Duiing this attack the Indians filled up the spring with sand and the defendeis of the foit had to dig for watei. Fiie-aiiows, shot at the combustible wooden buildings, were pievented by the iain fiom doing damage. Scouting paities of Indians remained neai the fort, and on Fiiday began the second attack.

"At about one o'clock in the afteinoon, dismounting and leaving theii ponies a mile distant, with demoniac yells the savages suiiounded the foit and at once commenced a fuiious musketiy fiie. The gaiiison ietuined the fiie with equal vigoi and with gieat effect on the yelling demons, who at first hoped by foice of numbeis to effect a quick entiance and had exposed themselves by a bold advance. This was soon checked.

" Little Crow's plan in this attack, in case the first

dash from all sides proved unsuccessful, was to pour a heavy continuous fire into the fort from every direction, exhausting the garrison as much as possible, and to carry the fort later by assault upon the south-west corner. To this end he collected the greater portion of his forces in that quarter, and, taking possession of the government stables and sutler's store, the fire literally riddled the buildings at that angle. It was found necessary to shell these buildings to dislodge the foe, resulting in their complete destruction by fire.

"Attempts were made to fire the fort by means of burning arrows but, the roofs being damp from recent rains, all efforts to this end were futile. Still, in pursuance of the plan of battle, the hail of bullets, the whizzing of arrows, and the blood-curdling war-whoop were incessant. . . .

"Now began the convergence to the southwest, the Indians passing from the opposite side in either direction. In moving around the northwest corner a wide detour was necessary to avoid McGrew's range, but the open prairie rendered the movement plainly apparent. Divining its object, McGrew hastily reported to Jones what was transpiring, and was authorized to bring out the twenty-four pounder, still in park, with which McGrew went into position on the west line of the fort and at the south of the commissary building. Meanwhile the fire in front of Jones' gun had become so hot and accurate as to splinter almost every lineal foot of timber along the top of his barricades, but he still returned shells at the shortest possible range.

"During an interval in the fusillade, Little Crow was heard urging, in the impassioned oratory of battle, the assault on the position. Jones doubly charged his piece with canister and reserved his fire; meanwhile McGrew had fired one shot from the twenty-four pounder at the party passing around the northeast, and training his gun westerly, dropped his second shell at the point where the party had by this time joined the reserve of squaws, ponies and dogs west of the main body. A great stampede resulted; the gun was swung to the left, bringing its line of fire between the two bodies of Indians. Its ponderous reverberations echoed up the valley as though twenty guns had opened, while the frightful explosion of its shells struck terror to the savages and effectually prevented a consolidation of the forces.

"At this juncture, Jones depressed his piece and fired close to the ground, killing and wounding seventeen savages of the party who had nerved themselves for the final assault. Completely demoralized by this unexpected slaughter, firing suddenly ceased and the attacking party precipitately withdrew, their hasty retreat attended by bursting shells until they were beyond range of the guns.

"Thus, after six hours of continuous blazing conflict, alternately lit up by the flames of burning buildings and darkened by whirling clouds of smoke, terminated the second and last attack.

"During the engagement, many of the men becoming short of musketry ammunition, spherical

case shot were opened in the barracks and women
worked with busy hands, making cartridges, while
men cut nail rods into short pieces to use as bullets.
The dismal whistling of these latter missiles was as
terrifying to the savages as were their fiendish yells
to the garrison.   Incredible as it may appear, during these engagements at Fort Ridgely the loss of
the garrison was only three men killed and thirteen wounded."

THE BIRCH COULIE MASSACRE.

Coulie is the name given by the early French *royageurs* to a ravine with a small stream of running water. Such a ravine exists as a dent in the wall of the Minnesota " bottoms," a short distance down the river from the present village of Morton. In August, 1862, there was plenty of water running down the coulie and plenty of wood near by for fires, so the fatigued party from Fort Ridgely and its escort, under command of Maj. Joseph R. Brown, chose this place for their camp, in spite of the many lurking places afforded by the woods and the ravine to any Indians who might be near.

The camp was in the regulation form, the army wagons being arranged in a circle, with the horses picketed outside, and the men sleeping inside the circle. Some of the men slept in tents and some

107

under the wagons rolled in their blankets, but all laid down with their loaded guns ready at hand. No new signs of Indians had been met, although the scenes of desolation through which they passed were a continual reminder to the soldiers of the blood-thirsty red men; with but little fear, therefore, the men laid down to rest, some of them to sleep their last sleep on earth.

"About four o'clock in the morning," says Lieut. J. J. Egan, who was present, "I heard a shot, and the next thing I heard was the cry, 'Indians!' and Captain Anderson yelling at his men, 'Lie on your bellies and shoot!'" Ten thousand muskets seemed to be going off. The men were stunned, the horses frightened, and terror and fear seized hold of us all. We blazed away in return, without aim or other object than to give evidence that there were survivors of their murderous fire, and to prevent a charge on the camp.

"As the red early dawn, covering everything with a halo of gold, revealed to our gaze what we supposed to be two thousand Indians surrounding us on all sides, their leaders mounted on horses caparisoned with gay colors, and themselves radiant in feathers, war paint, and all the bright and brilliant habiliments of Indian chiefs, the scene seemed unreal, as if a page had been torn from the leaves of the history of the crusades and the Saracen chiefs of. the plains of Asia transplanted to the new world. The fiercest yells and war-whoops, the shaking of blankets, the waving of flags to indicate new plans of movements of attack, the riding of horsemen here and there, were right before us, within about five hundred yards. Large bodies of Indians running continually, seeking new points of vantage, and taking orders from a chief, and all yelling and beating drums, made the scene unearthly. A shower of bullets continually fell upon us from all sides.

"The nature of the ground was such, with the coulie or ravine on one side, where was a heavy growth of timber, and the rest an open prairie with little hillocks here and there, just beyond our camp, the Indians could pour in a fire on us from every direction and themselves be protected. Men were dead and dying in the small circle of our encampment; the horses were nearly all killed in the first half hour, and it looked as if our last hour on earth had come. To be scalped and quartered, our hearts cut out, gave us no comforting reflections. Several of the men went crazy, and jumping out to give a full view, instantly met death.

"We then began to dig, each man for himself, his grave, as he expected. Three spades and one shovel were all the implements that could be found for use, but sabers and pocket knives were utilized, and about noon we had dug holes in the ground that afforded some protection. Never for an instant did the firing on us cease. Suddenly some one would drop his musket and roll over to die.

"About one o'clock in the afternoon, we heard a loud report like that of a cannon. We were all startled, not knowing whence the sound came.

Could the Indians have captured a howitzer? And did they have artillerists among them to turn it upon us? Again it boomed. Could it be possible we were saved? We were sixteen miles from Fort Ridgely, and how could knowledge of our situation have reached the fort?

"The silence of death prevailed in the camp. The movements of the Indians began to indicate something new, and after awhile, again the boom of the cannon sounded in our ears, and simultaneously every man jumped to his feet and gave a heartfelt hurrah. The spirit of audacity we exhibited led to a renewed fire upon us, and we speedily sought our respective places of safety. That afternoon we did not hear the cannon again, and night coming on, all hope of relief left our breasts, and each man sullenly and silently pursued his own meditations. It was a night of black despair. There seemed no hope. The cup of salvation had been snatched from our lips, and there was nothing to do but die.

"We expected to be starved to death, as any one

bold enough to raise up and put an arm into a wagon containing supplies were instantly shot. Our ammunition was almost exhausted, and each man laid his drawn saber near him and examined his musket, resolved not to fire again until the final moment came, when firing would do some execution. It happened to be quite dark also, which added to the uncertainties of the night. The agony we suf-- fered through the long, long night, expecting every moment to be rushed upon, is indescribable. Each moment seemed hours and hours, eternity. A soli- tary camp-fire at Gray Bird's headquarters partly relieved the gloom, and the blanketed specters stalk- ing ever and anon in front of that fire seemed ' ghosts or spirits of goblins damned.'

"Gladly we hail the morn gilding the horizon. We saw unusual movements among our enemy. Their war-whoops were fiercer, and their cries and gestures more frequent and emphatic. We expected the final hour had come and were prepared. The agony had been so intense that we felt a relief at the anticipated blow — no dread of death now lingered in the heart of any. Suddenly the boom of the cannon is again heard, and again, nearer and clearer, until its roar, usually terrible, sounded as the sweetest harmony of heaven. Confusion seems to pervade our enemies; they are in full flight. But we do not move from our holes until General Sibley, with a few officers, came right up to us, and then, and not till then, did we feel we were saved.

"Saved! Yes, and from a fearful death; and yet dying might have been less terrible than living. For thirty hours the soldiers had been under fire, and tasted neither food nor water. Twenty-three of their number lay stark and dead in the little encampment; forty-five others were wounded and groaning and crying for water.

"General Sibley. had heard the firing at Fort Ridgely on the morning of Sept. 2, and had sent out a party under Colonel McPhail, and then had followed with the entire command.

"Time will magnify the significance of this Birch

Coulie battle, and it will be remembered that it was fought by men without experience in war, those who had just enlisted in the service and those who had never enlisted, but who, on the first signal of danger, left their stores and other places of occupation, taking their lives in their hands for the protection of their people and the state."

THE OUTCOME.

Under the command of Colonel (afterwards Brig-adier-General) Sibley, a sharp campaign was immediately begun against the Indians concerned in the outbreak. Of the prisoners taken, four hundred and twenty-five were tried by court-martial, and of this number three hundred and twenty-one were found guilty. Three hundred and three of these were sentenced to be hanged, but in the following order the President commuted the sentences in the case of all but thirty-nine:

Executive Mansion,

Washington, D.C., Dec. 6, 1862.

Brig.-Gen. Henry H. Sibley,

St. Paul, Minn.:—

Ordered, that of the Indians and half-breeds sentenced to be hanged by the military commission, you cause to be executed on Fiiday, the nineteenth day of Decembei, instant, the following named, to wit: White Day, Tazoo . . .

The othei condemned piisoheis you will hold, subject to fuithei oideis, taking caie that they neithei escape noi are subjected to any unlawful violence.

ABRAHAM LINCOLN,
President of the United States.

THEIR LAST DAY UPON EARTH.

(From a newspaper, 1862.)

Wednesday, the 24th of December, was set apart for the interviews between the condemned and such of their relatives and friends as were confined in the main prison. Each Indian had some word to send to his parents or family. When speaking of their wives and children, almost everyone was affected to tears. Good counsel was sent to the children. Most of them spoke confidently of their hopes of salvation.

There is a ruling passion with Indians, and Tazoo could not refrain from its enjoyment, even in this sad hour. Tatimima was sending word to his relatives not to mourn his loss; he said he was old and could not hope to live long under any circumstances, and his execution would not shorten his days a great

117

WA-KAN-O-ZHAN-ZHAN.

deal, and dying as he did, innocent of any white man's blood, he hoped would give him a better chance to be saved; therefore, he hoped his friends would consider his death but as a removal from this to a better world.

"I have every hope," said he, "of going direct to the abode of the Great Spirit, where I shall always be happy."

This last remark reached the ears of Tazoo, who was also speaking to his friends, and he elaborated upon it in this wise:

"Yes, tell our friends that we are being removed from this world over the same path they must shortly travel. We go first, but many of our friends will follow us in a short time. I expect to go direct to the abode of the Great Spirit and be happy when I get there; but we are told that the road is long and the distance great; therefore, as I am slow in all my movements, it will probably take me a long time to reach the end of the journey, and I should not be surprised if some of the young, active men we will leave behind will pass me on the road before I reach the place of my destination."

In shaking hands with Red Iron and Akipa, Tazoo said, "Friends, last summer you were opposed to us. You were living in continual apprehension of an attack from those who were determined to exterminate the whites. Yourselves and families were subjected to many taunts, insults, and threats; still you stood firm in your friendship for the whites, and continually counselled the Indians to abandon their raids against them. Your course was condemned at the time, but now we see your wisdom. You were right when you said that the whites could not be exterminated, and the attempt indicated folly. Then you and your families were prisoners, and the lives of all in constant danger. To-day you are at liberty, assisting in feeding and guarding us; and thirty-nine men will die in two days because they did not follow your example and advice."

On Thursday evening the ordinance of baptism was solemnized by the Catholic priest present, and received by a considerable number of the condemned. Some of them entered into the ceremony with an apparently earnest feeling and an intelligent sense of its solemn character; all seemed resigned to their fate and depressed in spirits. Most of those not participating in the ceremony sat motionless and more like statues than living men.

On Friday morning, we accompanied the Rev. Father Ravoux to the prison of the condemned. He spoke to them of their condition and fate and in such terms as the devoted priest only can speak. He tried to infuse them with courage, bade them to hold out bravely and be strong, and to show no sign of fear. While Father Ravoux was speaking to them, old Tazoo broke out in a death-wail in which one after another joined until the prison room was filled with a wild, unearthly plaint, which was neither of despair nor grief, but rather a paroxysm of savage passion, most impressive to witness and startling to hear, even to those who understood the language of the music only. During the lulls of their death-song they would resume their pipes and, with the exception of an occasional mutter, or the rattling of their chains, they sat motionless and impassive, until one among the elder would break out in a wild wail, when all would join again in the solemn preparation for death.

Following this, the Rev. Dr. Williamson addressed them in their native tongue; after which they broke out again in their song of death. This last was thrilling beyond expression. The trembling voices, the forms shaking with passionate emotion, the half-uttered words through set teeth, all made up a scene which no one who saw can ever forget.

The influence of the wild music of their death-song upon them was almost magical. Their whole manner changed after they had closed their singing, and an air of cheerful unconcern marked all of them. It seemed as if during their passionate wailing they had passed in spirit through the valley of the shadow of death and already had their eyes fixed on the pleasant hunting-grounds beyond.

They had evidently taken great pains to make

themselves presentable for their last appearance on the stage of life. Most of them had little pocket-mirrors, and before they were bound employed themselves in putting on the finishing touches of paint, and arranging their hair according to the Indian mode. All had religious emblems, mostly crosses of fine silver or steel, and these were displayed with all the prominence of an exquisite or a *religeuse.* Many were painted in war style, with bands and beads and feathers, and were decked as gayly as for a festival. They expressed a desire to shake hands with the reporters who were to write about how they looked and acted, and with the artist who was to picture their appearance. This privilege was allowed them. Nearly all, on shaking hands, would point their fingers to the sky and say, as plainly as they could, "Me going up." White Day told us it was Little Crow who got them into the scrape, and now *they* had to die for it. One said there was a Great Spirit above who would take him home, and that he should die happy.

At a little after nine o'clock A.M., the Rev. Father Ravoux entered the prison again to perform the closing religious exercises. The guard fell back as he came in, the Indians ranging themselves around the room. The father addressed the condemned at some length and appeared much affected. He then knelt on the floor in their midst and prayed with them, all following and uniting with him in an audible voice. They appeared like a different race of beings while going through these religious exercises. Their voices were low and humble, and every exhibition of Indian bravado was banished.

While Father Ravoux was speaking to the Indians and repeating for the hundredth time his urgent request, that they must think to the last of the Great Spirit before whom they were about to appear, Provost Marshal Redfield entered and whispered a word in the ear of the good priest, who immediately said a word or two in French to Henry Milord, a half-breed, who repeated it in Dakota to the Indians, who were all lying down around the prison. In a moment eveiy Indian stood eiect, and as the Piovost Maishal opened the dooi, they fell in behind him with the gieatest alaciity. Indeed, a notice of ielease, paidon, oi iepiieve could not have induced them to leave the cell with moie appaient willingness than this call to death.

At the top of the steps theie was no delay. Captain Redfield mounted the diop at the head, and the Indians ciowded aftei him as if it weie a iace to see who would get up fiist. They actually ciowded on each othei's heels, and as they got to the top each took his position without any assistance fiom those who had been detailed for that puipose. They still kept up a mouinful wail, and occasionally theie would be a pieicing scieam.

The iopes weie soon aiianged aiound theii necks, not the least iesistance being offeied. The white caps which had been placed on the top of theii heads weie now diawn down ovei theii faces, shutting out foievei the light of day. Then ensued a scene that can haidly be desciibed, and which can nevei be forgotten. All joined in shouting and singing, as it appeared to those who were ignorant of the language. The tones seemed somewhat discordant, yet there was harmony in it. Save the instant of cutting the rope, it was the most thrilling moment of the awful scene. And it was not their voices alone. Their bodies swayed to and fro, and their every limb seemed to be keeping time.

The most touching scene on the drop was their attempt to grasp each other's hands, fettered as they were. They were very close to each other and many succeeded. Three or four in a row were hand in hand, all hands swaying up and down with the rise and fall of their voices. One old man reached out on each side, but could not grasp a hand; his struggles were piteous and affected many beholders.

We were informed by those who understood the language that their singing and shouting was only to sustain each other — that there was nothing defiant in their last moments, and that no death-song, strictly speaking, was chanted on the gallows.

Each one shouted his own name, and called on the name of his friend, saying in substance, "I'm here! I'm here!"

Captain Burt hastily scanned all the arrangements for the execution and motioned to Major Brown, the signal officer, that all was ready. There was one tap of the drum, almost drowned by the voices of the Indians — another, and the stays of the drop were knocked away, the rope cut, and with a crash down came the drop.

CHAS. E. FLANDRAU.
(Defender of New Ulm.)

INDIAN STRATEGY.*

ON THE YELLOW MEDICINE, 1856.

One day, after skirmishing about over considerable country, we made a camp on the Yellow Medicine River, near a fine spring, and everything seemed comfortable. The formation of the camp was a square with the guns and tents inside, and a sort of picket line on all sides about a hundred yards from the center, on which the sentinels marched day and night.

I tented with the Major, and seeing that the Indians were allowed to come inside the picket lines with their guns in their hands, I took the liberty of saying to him that I did not consider such a policy safe, because the Indians could, at a

---

* By kind permission of the publisher. E. W. Porter, this story and the following one are reproduced here from "Tales of the Frontier," by Judge C. E. Flandrau.

conceited signal, each pick out his man and shoot him down, and then where would the battery be?

But the Major's answer was, "Oh, we must not show any timidity."

So I said no more, but it was just such misplaced confidence that afterwards cost General Canby his life among the Modocs, when he was shot down by Captain Jack.

Things went on quietly, until one day a young soldier went down to the spring with his bucket and dipper for water, and an Indian who desired to make a name for himself among his fellows, followed him stealthily, and when he was in a stooping posture, filling his bucket, came up behind him, and plunged a long knife into his neck, intending of course to kill him; but as luck would have it, the knife struck his collar-bone and doubled up, so the Indian could not withdraw it. The shock nearly prostrated the soldier, but he succeeded in reaching camp. The Major immediately demanded the surrender of the guilty party, and he was given up by the Indians. I noticed one thing, however; no more Indians were allowed inside the lines with their guns in their hands.

When the prisoner was brought into camp, a guard tent was established and he was confined in it, with ten men to stand guard over him. These men were each armed with a Minie rifle, which was first introduced into the army and which was quite an effective weapon.

While all this was going on, we were holding pow-wows every day with the Indians, endeavoring to straighten out and clear up all the vexed questions between us. The manner of holding the council was to select a place on the prairie, plant an American flag in the center, and all hands squat down in a circle around it. Then the speechifying would commence, and last for hours without any satisfactory result. Anyone who has had much experience in Indian councils is aware of the hopelessness of arriving at a termination of the discussion. It very much resembles Turkish diplomacy.

But the weather was pleasant and every one
was patient.

The Indians, however, were concocting plans all
this time to effect the escape of the prisoner in
the guard-house. So one day they suggested a
certain place for the holding of the council, giving
some plausible reason for the change of location,
and when the time arrived, everybody assembled,
and the ring was formed.

Those present consisted of all the traders, Superintendent Cullen, Major Sheehan, Lieutenant Ayer,
in fact all the white men at the agency, and about
one hundred Indians, every one of whom had a gun
in his hands. I had warned the Major frequently
not to allow an Indian to come to council with a
gun, but he deemed it better not to show any timidity, and so they were not prohibited.

The council on this occasion was held about four
hundred yards from the battery camp, and on lower
grounds, but with no obstructions between them.
The scheme of the savages was to spring to their

feet on a conceited signal and begin firing their guns all around the council circle, so as to create a great excitement and bring everyone to their feet, and just at this moment the prisoner in the guard-house was to make a run in the direction of the council, keeping exactly between the guard and the whites in the council ring, believing the soldiers would not fire for fear of killing their own people.

When the time arrived every Indian jumped to his feet and fired in the air, creating a tremendous fusillade, and as had been expected, the most frightful panic followed, and everyone thinking that a general massacre of the whites had begun, they scattered in all directions. Instantly the prisoner ran for the crowd, and an Indian can sprint like a deer. Contrary to expectations, every one of the ten guards opened fire on him, and seven of them hit him, but curiously not one of the wounds stopped his progress and he got away; but the bullets went over and among the whites, one ricochetting through the coat of Major Cullen.

The prisoner never was caught, but I heard a great deal of him afterwards. His exploit of stabbing the soldier and his almost miraculous escape made him one of the most celebrated medicine men of his band, and he continued to work wonders thenceforth.

PUG–ON–A–KE–SHIG AND THE BATTLE OF LEECH LAKE.

(By C. E. Flandrau.)

Early in October, 1898, there was an Indian battle fought at Leech Lake, in this state, the magnitude of the result of which gives it a place in the history of Minnesota, although it was strictly a matter of United States cognizance and jurisdiction. In Cass county there is a Chippewa Indian reservation, and like all other Indian reservations, there are to be found there turbulent people, both white and red.

There is a large island out in Leech Lake, called Bear Island, which is inhabited by the Indians. On October 1, 1897, one Indian shot another on the island. A prominent member of the tribe named Pug-on-a-ke-shig (Hole in the Day) was present and witnessed the shooting. An indictment was found in the United States district court against the Indian who did the shooting, but before any trial could be had the matter was settled by the Indians in their own way, and they thought that was the last of it. A subpœna was issued for Pug-on-a-ke-shig and a deputy marshal served it. He disregarded the subpœna. An attachment was then issued to arrest him and bring him into court. A deputy United States marshal tried to serve it, and was resisted by the Indian and his friends on three different occasions, and once when the Indian was arrested he was rescued from the custody of the marshal — warrants were then issued for the arrest of twenty-one of the rescuers.

This was in the latter part of August, 1898. Troops were asked for to aid the marshal in making his arrests, and a lieutenant and twenty men were sent from Fort Snelling for that purpose. . . . It soon became apparent that there would be trouble before the Indians could be brought to terms, and General Bacon, the officer in command of the Department of Dakota, with headquarters at

St. Paul, oideied Majoi Wilkinson of Company "E," of the Thiid Regiment of United States Infantiy, stationed at Foit Snelling, with his company of eighty men to the scene of the tioubles. Geneial Bacon accompanied these tioops. On the 5th of Octobei, 1898, the whole foice left Walkei in boats for a place on the east bank of the lake, called Sugai Point, wheie theie was a cleaiing of seveial acies and a log house, occupied by Pug-on-a-ke-shig.

When the command landed, only a few squaws and Indians weie visible. The deputy maishals landed, and, with the inteipieteis, went at once to the house, and while theie discoveied an Indian whom Colonel Sheehan iecognized as one for whom a waiiant was out, and immediately attempted to aiiest and handcuff him. The Indians iesisted vigoiously, and it was only with the aid of thiee or foui soldieis that they succeeded in aiiesting him. He was put on boaid of the boat. The whole foice then skiimished thiough the timbei in seaich of Indians, and did not believe there were any in the vicinity, when in fact the Indians had watched their every movement, and were close to their trail, waiting for the most advantageous moment to strike. It was the same tactics which the Indians had so often adopted with much success in their warfare with the whites. While stacking arms, a new recruit allowed his gun to fall to the ground, and it was discharged accidentally.

The Indians were silently awaiting their opportunity, supposing it was the signal of attack, opened fire on the troops, and a vicious battle began. The soldiers seized their arms and returned the fire as best they could, directing it at the point whence came the shots from the invisible enemy, concealed in the dense thicket. The battle raged for several hours. General Bacon, with a gun in his hands, was everywhere, encouraging the men. Major Wilkinson, as cool as if he had been in a drawing-room, cheered his men on, but was thrice wounded, the last hit proving fatal. Colonel Sheehan iustinctively entered.the fight and took chaige of the light wing of the line, chaiging the enemy with a few followeis and keeping up a iapid fiie. The iesult of the fight was six killed and nine wounded on the pait of the tioops. No estimate has evei been satisfactoiily obtained of the loss of the enemy.

Latei the United States commissionei of Indian affaiis aiiived on the scene and satisfactoiily settled with the Indians.

THE GRASSHOPPER SCOURGE IN RENVILLE COUNTY.

(Written by County Supt. Eric Ericson, Olivia, Minn., for this publication.)

The great grasshopper scourge in southern Minnesota assumed serious proportions in 1874, and the locusts increased in numbers and destructiveness until the early summer of 1878, when they disappeared. The first year, the hatching of the locusts and the work of destruction in Renville county, was confined to the sandy soil along the Minnesota river, in the townships of Flora and Sacred Heart.

It is not known from where the vanguard came — probably from the arid regions of the southwest. They multiply with great rapidity, the eggs being laid late in the summer, in packets of about seventy-five, in holes bored in the ground. The locust is exceedingly voracious, which may be explained by reference to its alimentary canal, which is highly

140

developed, the gizzard being provided with from six
to eight rows of horny denticulated plates situated
on ridges, the whole number of teeth in some
species amounting to 270. The stomach and sali-
vary glands are highly developed, the large jaws
further adapting it for its vegetable diet. The air-
tubes dilate into numerous large air-reservoirs,
which assist it in taking its long-sustained flights.
The young are hatched about May, and at once
begin their work of devouring the tender grain.
They move along in solid phalanx over a field of
grain, eating everything clean as they go. The
myriads stretching across the field, the township,
the county, made it a hopeless task to exterminate
them. Many devices were tried, such as plowing
and burning, but no perceptible impression was
made.

About July 1 they acquire wings and fly in great
swarms from place to place. These flights are
taken during the middle of the day, usually at a
height of 200 to 300 feet, and when watched, as

they usually weie, by the stiuggling and anxious settleis of those eaily times, to whom a ciop was theii all, theii tianspaient wings made them look like snow flakes, and they seemed almost as numeious. Between foui oi five o'clock they would light, usually in fields of giain, eat the juicy stalks and heads of the giain, and destioy all in a few houis. In 1876 and 1877 the entiie county was liteially coveied with locusts, the fields of giain being swept clean fiom one end to the othei. The wiitei has seen houses black with locusts, and tiees so heavily loaded with them that the bianches swayed and bent with theii weight.

In 1876, eleven counties weie filled with giasshoppei eggs. The legislatuie passed a iesolution iecommending that the piaiiies be buined, at a ceitain time of the yeai, so as to destioy the eggs and the young. They also memoiialized Congiess to giant aid to those who had theii ciops destioyed yeai aftei yeai.

In those days people lived in sod shanties, oi

houses built of cheap lumber, and little of it. Fur coats were almost unknown. Very many families lived on cheap, coarse bread, with little meat or butter. Groceries were a luxury. The nearest market places were New Ulm and Willmar until the fall of 1878. Many of the early settlers returned to the east, some to come back after the grasshoppers had finally disappeared, others, not.

The United States government sent out army clothing and a lieutenant of the regular army distributed it to the needy. The state of Minnesota appropriated money to help the people get seed grain, Renville county receiving $12,000 from the appropriation made by the legislature in January, 1878. The state also sent out hundreds of barrels of coal tar which was spread upon large tin plates, or any flat surface of considerable length and breadth, which was dragged over the field of grain. The young hoppers would jump upon this platform as it was moved along and be caught in the tar. Tons of them were destroyed, for the fight was a despeiate one to get biead for the family of little ones, and a fiaction of the giowing giain was, in some cases, saved. Seed peas weie also fuinished by the state, and patches of gieatei oi less extent planted. The festive hoppei did not seem to caie for this diet, and many a faimei's family gladly dined on pea soup.

In the summei of 1878 the hoppeis took flight befoie depositing any eggs and whithei they went was a mysteiy. It was fiimly believed, howevei, that they would hatch somewheie else and ietuin thickei than evei the next year. The outcome was awaited with almost bated bieath, and the ielief was gieat when the hoppeis failed to again appeai. But even theii failuie to appeai that yeai did not at once quiet foiebodings. People believed the coun- tiy would be visited peiiodically by these pests, and a few yeais at the most was all the exemption that could be expected. Happily these foiebodings have not been fulfilled, and we hope nevei will be.

MINNESOTA IN THE WAR WITH SPAIN.

On the 25th of April, 1898, Congress passed an act declaring that war against Spain had existed since the 21st of the month. A requisition was made on Minnesota for its quota of troops immediately after war was declared, and late in the afternoon of the twenty-eighth day of April the Governor issued an order to the adjutant-general to assemble the state troops in St. Paul.

The order was promptly obeyed, and all the field, staff and company officers, with their commands, reported before the time appointed, and on the afternoon of that day went into camp at the state fair ground, which was named Camp Ramsey.

Minnesota, in 1861, was the first state to offer troops for service in the Civil War and in 1898 again gained that proud distinction. Her soldiers,

145

of the Thirteenth Regiment, served with distinction in the Philippines, being engaged in many battles in the islands, finally returning home to be mustered out October 12, 1899, in St. Paul, being reviewed by our late lamented President McKinley and several of his cabinet.

SCENE IN MILLING DISTRICT IN MINNEAPOLIS.

HUNTING WOLVES IN BED.*

ON THE MINNESOTA RIVER, 1854.

Garvie and I had gotten quietly settled in our
shanty on the prairie, when one excessively cold
night an Indian boy, about thirteen years of age,
saw our light and came to the door, giving us to
understand that his people were encamped about
four or five miles up the river, and that he was
afraid to go any farther lest he should freeze to
death. He was mounted on a pony, had a pack
of furs with him, and asked us to take him in for
the night. We of course did so and made him as
comfortable as we could by giving him a buffalo
robe on the floor. But we had no shelter for the
pony, and all we could do was to hitch him on the
lee side of the shanty and strap a blanket on him.

* Reproduced from " Tales of the Frontier " by permission of Judge C. E. Flandrau, and the publisher, E. W. Porter, St. Paul.

When morning came he was frozen to death. We got the poor little boy safely off on the way to his people's camp, and decided to utilize the carcass of the pony for wolf bait.

In order to present an intelligent idea of the situation, I will say that the river made an immense detour in front of the shanty, having a large extent of bottom land, covered with a dense chapparral, which was the home of thousands of wolves, and as soon as night came they would start out in droves in search of prey.

We hauled the dead pony out to the back of the shanty and left it about two rods distant from the window. The moment night set in, the wolves in packs would attack the carcass. At first we would step outside and fire into them with buckshot from double-barreled shot-guns, but we found they were so wary that the mere movement of opening the door to get out would frighten them, and we had very limited success for the first few nights. Another difficulty we encountered was shooting in the daik. If you have never tried it, and ever do, you will find it exceedingly difficult to get any kind of an aim, and you will have to fire at the sound rather than the object.

We remedied this trouble, however, by taking out a light of glass from the back window, and building a rest that bore directly on the carcass, so that we could poke our guns through the opening, settle them on the rest, and blaze away into the gloom. We brought our bed up to the window so that we could shoot without getting out of it, while snugly wrapped up in our blankets. After this our luck improved, and after each dischaige we would rush out, and with a tomahawk, despatch the wounded wolves and collect the dead ones, until we had slaughtered forty-two of them. We skinned them and sold the pelts to traders for seventy-five cents a piece, which money was the first of our earnings.

THE FALLS OF MINNEHAHA IN WINTER

THE FALLS OF MINNEHAHA.

This was Hiawatha's wooing!
Thus it was he won the daughter
Of the ancient Arrow-maker,
In the land of the Dacotahs!
  From the wigwam he departed,
Leading with him Laughing Water;
Hand in hand they went together,
Through the woodland and the meadow,

Left the old man standing lonely
At the doorway of his wigwam,
Heard the falls of Minnehaha
Calling to them from the distance,
Crying to them from afar off,
" Fare thee well, O Minnehaha! "
    And the ancient Arrow-maker
Turned again unto his labor,
Sat down by his sunny doorway,
Murmuring to himself, and saying:
" Thus it is our daughters leave us,
Those we love and those who love us!
Just when they have learned to help us,
When we are old and lean upon them,
Comes a youth with flaunting feathers,
With his flute of reeds, a stranger
Wanders piping through the village,
Beckons to the fairest maiden,
And she follows where he leads her,
Leaving all things for the stranger! "

                    — Longfellow.